Jimmy's Boa
and the
Bungee Jump
Slam Dunk

BASKETBALL
PRACTICE

Lesson One
THE DRIBBLE

Dial Books for Young Readers  New York

Jimmy's Boa and the Bungee Jump Slam Dunk

Welcome
to
Miss Peachtree's
School
of the
Dance

BASKETBALL
PRACTICE
Lesson One
THE DRIBBLE

by Trinka Hakes Noble
pictures by Steven Kellogg

For Erica and Tom, with love
—T.H.N.

To Peter the Great, with love
—S.K.

Published by Dial Books for Young Readers
A division of Penguin Young Readers Group
345 Hudson Street, New York, New York 10014
Text copyright © 2003 by Trinka Hakes Noble
Pictures copyright © 2003 by Steven Kellogg
All rights reserved
Designed by Lily Malcom
Text set in Zapf International
Printed in the U.S.A. on acid-free paper
1 3 5 7 9 10 8 6 4 2
Library of Congress Cataloging-in-Publication Data
Noble, Trinka Hakes.
Jimmy's boa and the bungee jump slam dunk / by Trinka Hakes Noble ;
pictures by Steven Kellogg.
p. cm.
Summary: Jimmy's boa constrictor creates havoc in his gym class and
his antics lead to the formation of an unusual basketball team.
ISBN 0-8037-2600-7
[1. Boa constrictor—Fiction. 2. Snakes as pets—Fiction. 3. Schools—Fiction.
4. Basketball—Fiction.] I. Kellogg, Steven, ill.
II. Title.
PZ7.N6715 Jhe 2003
[E]—dc21   2002004000

The artwork was prepared using ink and pencil line,
watercolor washes, and acrylic paints.

"Hi, Meggie. How was basketball practice?"

"A real bummer . . . until Jimmy's boa saved the day."
"His boa? What was Jimmy's pet boa constrictor doing
  there?"

Lesson One

THE WALTZ

"Dancing with Jimmy."

"Dancing?"

"Yeah. Miss Peachtree took over the gym for her dance school. Jimmy refused to dance with anyone but his boa, so I had to dance with Peaches, Miss Peachtree's poodle. But when Miss Peachtree tried to teach us the tangle—"

Lesson Two: THE TANG

"Uh, Meggie, don't you mean the tango?"

"Not when Jimmy's boa is dancing. His tail was so long that we got all tangled up. Miss Peachtree got mad and said he had two left feet."

"Jimmy?"

"No, his boa.

"And I think it hurt the boa's feelings, because he climbed up in one of the baskets and wouldn't come down. So Jimmy tried to coax him out with a basketball."

"Did it work?"   "Not really.

"Jimmy's boa took the ball and whipped it downcourt for a long shot.

"So Jimmy ran down, grabbed the rebound, and sunk a super hook shot. That's when Coach Carney came dancing out of his office."

BASKET-BALLET

"Coach Carney was dancing at Miss Peachtree's class?"
"Well, sort of, and it was a good thing too, because when
Miss Peachtree tried to take the basketball away from
Jimmy, the coach blew his whistle and called for a
jump ball."

"A jump ball between Miss Peachtree and Jimmy? But isn't Miss Peachtree taller and bigger than Jimmy?"

"No kidding, Mom, and she even had on high heels!

"Coach let Jimmy use the trampoline, but Miss Peachtree said that wasn't fair.

"So Jimmy's boa came down and made himself into a spring to give her extra lift."

"Did the boa help her out?"

"Yeah, way out! She never came down. So Jimmy tipped the ball to me and I waltzed it to Tommy, who swung Jenny downcourt for a layup shot. Then Marianne and Jerome hip-hopped the ball out to Miss Peachtree's chauffeur, Dobson, who scored from downtown!"

"Why, Meggie, I'm so impressed!"

"So was the coach. He said he'd never seen such fancy footwork. He got so excited that he threw the ball up in the air and shouted, 'YES! I HAVE A BASKETBALL TEAM!' But the ball never came down."
"It didn't? Was it stuck up in the rafters?"

"No, but Miss Peachtree was.

"Miss Peachtree caught the ball when she bungee jumped off the rafters

and slam-dunked it right through the basket."

"She WHAT? How'd she do THAT?!"
"With a little help from Jimmy's boa.
He was her bungee cord.

"Coach Carney thought Miss Peachtree's slam dunk was so
spectacular that he signed her up as our assistant coach.
But she told him to stuff it."

"Oh, dear. Was he mad?"
"No, glad. He thought she meant to stuff the basketball.
He said, 'That's the spirit, old girl.' Anyway, we couldn't
start practice right away."
"Oh no? Why not?"

"Because the gym was overrun with rabbits."
"Rabbits? What rabbits?"

"The ones living near our playground. When they heard all the bouncing, they peeked in the side door and were blown away by Miss Peachtree's super jump. Mom, those rabbits were all ears, wanting to know her jumping technique."
"Was she okay with that?"

"Yeah, I think so, because she said the rabbits should join our team.

"But Coach said no, there was only one space left and that was for Jimmy's boa."

"Why would he want that boa?"

"I think it has something to do with our team's name."
"Oh? What's your name?"

"The Scream Team."   "THE SCREAM TEAM?!"

"Yeah, and Coach said that with Jimmy's boa and his bungee jump slam dunk, we'll win every game!"

★ THE SCORE ★

| THE SCREAM TEAM | 325 |
| THE HOUNDS | 0 |

"My goodness, I guess that was the end of dance class, huh?"
"Not really, Mom. Tomorrow the rabbits are going to teach
  us the bunny hop so we can practice jumping. And that's
  why I've got to go over to Jimmy's to help."
"Oh, no. To help with what?"

"The rabbits. They all went home with Jimmy."
"I don't know how Jimmy's mom does it."
"Don't worry, Mom. You'll find out. I'm bringing Jimmy
  and the rabbits and the whole gang home for dinner!"

"Carrots, anyone?"